This Book Belongs To

_____

The Warm Hearted
Snowman

By: Sigal Adler

We all know there's magic that comes once a year,

When it snows and we know that Christmas is near,

In one tiny village all glowing with light,

A very grand snowman stood guard day and night.

The children all waited throughout the whole year

And when the snow fell, they'd give a great cheer,

Building the snowman with love and with pride,

Then waving goodbye and darting inside.

Yet still something's missing – a nose for his face!

The children all hurried, set a carrot in place.

The snowman felt proud of the one that they chose,

"For everyone knows that I need a nose"!

But when nighttime fell, the snowman would groan,

For the children must leave, and he'd be all alone;

The snowman stood there and talked with the moon,

Hoping for sunrise, when the kids would come soon.

Until he awoke one very bleak day,

His nose had gone missing, he saw with dismay.

"Now I look awful!" At least, so he thought

Until the kids stuck a new one in its spot.

Ah, life was good, what a wonderful time!

With all the kids jumping and trying to climb;

A day with a nose is just perfect with friends,

But as he well knew, all days have their ends.

And when night arrived, he stood there in the dark

No kids all around, no one in the park

For it was, so he knew, at last Christmas Eve

And all of his friends had to go home and leave.

Surrounded by love, with their families so warm,

Not caring that he stood alone in the storm.

He decided he wouldn't give in to his grief

Instead he would stay up and catch the nose thief!

So he stood with one eye half-open, aware

Didn't sleep for a second – no, he wouldn't dare.

He waited two hours, he waited for three,

He asked "Who is there?" The answer came: "Me!"

A small frightened bunny afraid on his head;

"Don't hurt me, please," that poor bunny said.

"I beg you, please," the small bunny pleaded,

"But listen, your carrot – well, it's truly needed!"

His parents had gotten lost deep in the snow,

And now here on Christmas he had nowhere to go.

"The winter's a hard time for rabbits," he said,

"So I took the carrot right off of your head."

And after the bunny had told his whole story,

He cried just a bit and he said he was sorry.

That good-hearted snowman saw the tears bunny cried

Looked at him kindly and then smiled wide;

"Take my nose, please, for I don't mind a bit,

"But perhaps you'll stay here a while and sit?

"I'll give you my nose for this kindness you've shown,

"Coming on Christmas as I stood here alone."

That bunny returned almost every night,

To visit his friend who was tall, cold, and white;

And each night he'd leave with the snowman's long nose

Enjoying the carrots the village kids chose.

The children would rush up each morning, excited,

Push in the new nose and then stand back, delighted;

They didn't mind doing it, thought it quite fun,

And each one felt happy when that job was done.

The kids thought the nose was just blowing away,

"It happened again!" they all loved to say,

Little suspecting the regular habit

Of their lovely snowman and his friend the rabbit.

But one chilly morning the bunny poked out one ear

He felt the sun warming up, gave a great cheer;

"Summer is coming, the sun's here at last!

And soon winter's freeze will be over and past!"

Hopping from one sun-warmed bush to the other,

He rounded the bend – and spotted his brother!

His parents were there, too; his mom and his dad,

And hugged them and told of the winter he'd had.

Back with his family, so pleased through and through,

The bunny knew he still had something to do;

So the next day he hopped down to his friend's place –

But the snowman had vanished and left not a trace!

All he saw was a carrot on a pile of snow,

And he wondered aloud, "Now, where did he go?"

The rabbit went home but he still felt so bad

Not thanking the very best friend that he'd had;

The warm-hearted snowman had saved him, no doubt,

Rescuing him when no-one was about.

Months passed, but that rabbit never forgot

And one day, the snow fell – then it fell quite a lot.

He knew it was Christmas from the songs in the air,

And the coats and the mittens the children would wear.

And hopping right by on his path through the town...

He spotted a friendly face winking down!

"Don't be sad, little rabbit; I'll come back each year,

To brighten the town and bring Christmas cheer!"

Adler.sigal@gmail.com

22330604R00029

Made in the USA
Middletown, DE
13 December 2018